Contents

Oldmoor Hall

Who would want to stay at Oldmoor Hall?

The old hotel was rickety and broken. Its roof leaked. Windows rattled. Mould crept through the wallpaper and mushrooms blossomed in the cellar. The whole building was leaning to the side, and the cracks in its walls opened wider every day.

It was also in the middle of nowhere. All around it, boggy moors stretched, bleak and desolate. And every day, drifting off those moors, came thick, soupy fog.

Who would want to stay in such a place? Anyone who did, most sensible folk agreed, had to be mad, or sad, or strange, or all three of those things put together.

But mad, sad, strange people exist. And some

1

of them came to stay at Oldmoor Hall.

A lonely road ran past the old hotel, curving out of the mist. Every now and then a Guest came wandering up it.

Why? What drew them towards this place? Nobody knew.

But come they did. People wandered up that road. They saw the hotel. Needing a room for the night, they opened the front door, and went in.

Into the rickety old hotel . . .

The Parrot Knows All

"DING!"

Ernest shot out of his chair. His polished shoes landed on the carpet and he stood in front of the mirror in his office, straightening his tie. The sound of the bell, down in the lobby, faded.

"A Guest!" he muttered.

He tidied his uniform. He squirted a wobbling blob of cream into his hand, and smoothed it into his hair. What a fine sight he was, he thought. So neat, so well-turned-out. Of course, he was also only twelve years old. But what did that matter?

He was the Manager-in-Chief of Oldmoor Hall.

"Ding-ding-ding!"

The boy marched out of his office, along the corridor and into the lift. Rattling the cage door shut, he plummeted five floors down. The door clanked open and a girl, slightly younger than him, stumbled in. Ernest's left eyebrow lifted.

The girl's name was Daisy, and she was the Head Housekeeper of the hotel. She was also Ernest's younger sister. He watched her as she

straightened her scruffy pinny and pulled a cobweb out of her tangled hair. He wrinkled his nose.

"You," he sniffed, "are late."

"Just press the button, Ernest," she snapped.

The Manager-in-Chief did so. They rocketed down to the ground floor, spilled out into the marble-floored lobby, and took up their positions, Ernest bowing, Daisy doing a clumsy curtsey. The bell that had summoned them sat on the counter, its chime still trembling in the musty air.

But no one was there.

"Hello?" said Ernest.

A blur of feathers. A cackle. A large pink-and-green parrot swooped down, landed on the bell and bounced on it, making it ring.

5

Then he flew off round the lobby, cawing with laughter.

"Ding! That got you! Ding-ding!"

"Not again," said Ernest.

The parrot, whose name was Samson, was hysterical by now. He looped-the-loop, let off a cackle of glee and slammed into a pillar in its delight.

"Drat that bird," said Daisy.

"Now then, *little* sister," said Ernest. "Remember whose pet he is."

The two children's gazes swivelled over to a large painting on the wall. It was of a kindly-looking woman, and on her shoulder sat a parrot, identical to Samson.

"Grandmama." Ernest dropped onto one knee. "How we miss you."

Daisy giggled at her brother. He looked SO serious.

Ernest and Daisy were orphans and the only parent they had ever known was the old woman in the picture. They were unsure whether or not she was their grandmother, but they knew she had raised them since birth, and cared for them lovingly at Oldmoor Hall.

"What can have happened to her?" muttered Ernest.

"It's a mystery," replied Daisy.

Samson fluttered onto Ernest's shoulder. The bird suddenly looked mournful, and Ernest stroked his feathers. It was a whole month since the children had woken up one morning and discovered that Grandmama had left them. Nothing had been heard from her since, apart from one postcard of the Sahara desert which Ernest and Daisy had cut into two halves, so that each had a piece of Grandmama to keep in their uniforms, next to their hearts.

"I may be away some time," the postcard said. "Take charge of the hotel. Look after the Guests. Ernest to be Manager-in-Chief. Daisy, Head Housekeeper. Any questions, ask Samson."

"How thoughtful," mused Ernest, "of our dear Grandmama to teach her parrot to speak, so that he can pass on her wisdom to us."

"A pity," said Daisy, "that he's also totally mad and keeps on playing practical jokes."

"Tsk," said Ernest, "we mustn't grumble."

"But really!" protested Daisy. "What about when he tore out and ate every page of that book about hotel management, before we had even had the chance to read it? That's the sort of thing I'm talking about."

"For the second time," said her brother. "Don't grumble."

The two children marched back into the lift, clanked up to the top floor, and stepped out onto a wobbly balcony. A rusty telescope was attached to the railings. Daisy tilted it into the fog which seemed to be getting thicker and thicker. Eerie winds shuddered. The moors groaned.

"Any sign of a Guest?" asked Ernest.

"Nope," said Daisy, peering up the lonely road that curved away from the hotel. "Not yet. But the mist is getting thicker and thicker."

Sooner or later there would be a Guest, Ernest mused. A Guest who, according to Grandmama's instructions, must be looked after.

If only she had told them just a little bit more about this strange old hotel. But she had never said anything much about Oldmoor Hall, and the truth was that Ernest and Daisy had never really shown much interest while growing up there. When they were little, they had been too busy playing with their toys during the day, or being tucked up in bed at night. More recently, Ernest had spent all his time reading books, while Daisy played endless games of hide-and-seek with Samson. They had hardly given a thought to what their Grandmama might be getting up to elsewhere in the hotel, and that was why they now knew so little about this strange place and the mysterious Guests who came here.

"Come on," said Ernest, his heels clicking together. "We've got work to do."

No point worrying. No point pondering why, or when, or how. "Take charge of the hotel. Look after the Guests." That's what Grandmama had said. That was what they would do.

Ernest tugged his sister's sleeve and the two children turned and stepped back into the hotel. This meant they didn't see, at the very end of the lonely road that led away from the hotel, a tiny shape appear out of the swirling mist.

A dot. Moving towards them.

Samson saw it. He fluttered down onto the balcony rail. He stood on one leg, and stuck his tongue out of his beak at a funny angle.

"A Guest!" he cawed, going cross-eyed.

Then he flapped off, giggling, into the gloom.

Secret Passages

Ernest and Daisy spent the next hour cleaning. Or rather, Ernest did. He pushed along his trolley, with its mops and brooms, and dusted mirrors, swept floors and wiped off mould. Finally, his duties completed, he headed over to the other side of the hotel, to see how his sister was getting on.

Daisy had done nothing at all. There was dust and mildew everywhere. She was also nowhere in sight. Ernest paced the corridors, calling out her name.

"Daisy?"

"Behind you, Ernest!"

Ernest spun round on his heel, nearly losing his balance. But the corridor was empty. A draught wafted out of a marble fireplace, that was all. He turned back and continued on his search.

"Boo!"

He spun back. The fireplace was swivelling out from the wall, and there on the other side, covered with dust, was a grinning Daisy.

"Got you!"

"I wish you'd stop messing about," muttered her brother.

Secret passages. They ran all over the hotel and there was nothing Daisy loved more than jumping out of them and surprising the Manager-in-Chief. No wonder she was so untidy and covered with cobwebs.

"Come and explore with me!" giggled Daisy. "We'll play hide-and-seek properly then!"

"Some of us have enough work to do cleaning *normal* passageways," said Ernest, "without getting involved in secret ones."

"That's what you *always* say." Daisy pulled a lever and the fireplace spun round again, swinging her back out even more covered with dust. "Why don't you just admit it, Ernie? You're actually afraid of the dark."

"I am no such thing," spluttered Ernest. "And don't call me Ernie—"

He froze, staring at his sister.

She froze too. They had both heard it.

"Ding!"

"It's Samson again," said Ernest, relaxing. "One of his tricks, that's all."

But Daisy pointed. Samson was perched on the mantelpiece. He looked dizzy from spinning round on the fireplace, but he too had heard it.

It was the unmistakeable sound of the bell, downstairs in the lobby.

Elsie Tulip

"W-w-welcome to Oldmoor Hall."

Ernest steadied his heart, which was pounding after the race down to the lobby. Reaching up to smooth his hair, he glared across at Daisy, who was still covered in cobwebs. Trying to make up for her, the neatly uniformed boy bowed, and smiled at their very first Guest.

She was a plump little lady, with messy, straggly brown hair. She wore a long, mud-splattered overcoat and was clutching a large leather suitcase. She looked as if she'd fallen down several rabbit holes on the moor, and every part of her seemed to be trembling.

"Madam?"

"May I have a . . . a . . . room . . .?"

Her arms were trembling. Her knees were trembling. Even the material of her coat was trembling, which meant that everything inside must be trembling too, Ernest thought. Most of all, her nose was trembling. It was a red quivering blur, like a volcano about to go off.

Ernest lurched back, but too late.

"A-A-A-A-A-A-A-CHOOOOOOO!"

The sneeze exploded into his face. He wiped himself and glared again at Daisy, who had ducked under the counter. He turned back to the Guest, who was stumbling about with a pink-spotted handkerchief held to her nose. He opened the reservations book, a pen in his hand.

"A room? Certainly . . ."

"A-A-A-A-A-A-A-CHOOOOOOO!"

Another sneeze, and Ernest was entirely drenched. Determined, he kept going.

"Bless you, ma'am. Now may I have a name . . ."

"Elsie Tulip!" wheezed the Guest, recovering. "I'm so sorry about this sneezing! But I have an allergy, you see! A-A-A-A-A-A-A . . ."

Ernest couldn't help stepping back, but as he did so, he saw there was no need. With tremendous effort, the Guest stifled the sneeze, her whole face clenched with concentration.

"An allergy . . ." she gasped, "so sorry . . ."

"What's an allergy?" hissed Daisy, as she clambered up from under the counter. "Do you know, Ernest?"

"Something that makes you sneeze," Ernest muttered out of the corner of his mouth. "Or itch, or come out in a rash if you come into contact with certain things." In his spare time, he was learning all the words in the dictionary, in order to sound clever and more like a Manager-in-Chief. He had only got as far as 'A', but as that was the first letter of 'Allergy', he knew what it meant. "Some people have allergies to flowers, for example. Or grass. Or . . ."

"Anything furry!" gasped Elsie Tulip. The trembling was beginning again. "I'm still recovering from seeing a rabbit nearly a week ago! The slightest whiff of any animal with fur makes me explode with sneezing! It takes me days to get over it! Days!"

"Oh dear," said Ernest. "How upsetting."

"You don't have any furry creatures here, do you?" Small glistening eyes flicked about. "I cannot possibly stay if you do!"

"Do feathers count as furry?" said Daisy, pointing up at Samson on the chandelier. He'd been having great fun doing back-flips every time Elsie Tulip sneezed. "Because we have a parrot," she added.

"No, feathers are alright," Elsie said. Her fists clenched the edge of the counter with the effort of holding back the next sneeze. "I'm so sorry to make a fuss, but it really is very important! If anything furry gets close . . . it has the most terrible . . . A-A-A-A-CHOOO!"

It was the most powerful sneeze of all. Ernest felt his hair sweep backwards with the sheer force of the explosion. He decided it might be best to show the Guest to her room.

"Room 405," he said, reaching up for the key. "Any luggage?"

The question had an extraordinary effect on Elsie Tulip. As soon as Ernest had asked it, she snatched up the large leather suitcase that was on the floor beside her. With incredible speed and strength, her arms wrapped around it and she backed away.

"No!" she said. "I mean, yes, I do have luggage! But no, I don't need anyone to carry it! Not at all! Just show me to my room immediately!"

How very odd, thought Ernest. He would have thought the Guest would *want* to have her luggage carried, after dragging it all the way to Oldmoor Hall. But perhaps all that sneezing had made Elsie Tulip a little jumpy, he decided. Anyway, it wasn't any of his business. If this Guest wanted to carry her own suitcase, that was fine by him.

"Very well," he said. "Please follow me."

He led Elsie Tulip, who was still snuffling and clutching her suitcase tighter than ever, to the lift. Together, they travelled up to the fourth floor, and along the corridor to Room 405.

"I hope you like your room?" the Manager-in-Chief said, as he opened the door and showed the Guest in.

"As long as I can have a little peace and quiet to recover from my dreadful allergy," said Elsie. "I'll be happy enough."

She swept straight past him, and slammed the door.

Afternoon Tea

At three o'clock, Daisy took charge in the kitchen. When Grandmama had disappeared, the two children had immediately agreed that Daisy would look after cooking the food, while Ernest would be in charge of serving it. It was a situation that pleased Daisy greatly. She loved the dingy kitchen at the bottom of the hotel, with its clever machinery and huge ovens, and spent many hours down there, leafing through Grandmama's old recipe books. She was also extremely fond of the tiny walled vegetable patch, just outside the kitchen door. Strange vegetables grew out there, surrounded by fog, and Daisy liked nothing better than to dig a few of them up and turn them into complicated stews.

But there was no need for stew, or any other vegetable dish, that afternoon. All Elsie wanted was a cup of tea, and Daisy threw herself into the task, using the kitchen's intricate system of ropes, trolleys and pulleys to lower the tea strainer, pour the water, and drop the cup onto the saucer. Proudly, she placed the steaming drink in a little lift in the corner of the kitchen and rattled it up to the corridor outside Room 405.

Serving the drink went less smoothly. Ernest presented the tray, but was met with yet another colossal sneeze. The cup flew off the tray and smashed into the wall, tea splattered all over Ernest, and he mumbled an apology and hurried away. Fortunately, Daisy was able to send up another cup of tea in no time at all, but this time Ernest just left it outside Elsie's door, knocking quietly to let her know it was there.

"It must be awful," said Daisy shortly after-wards, in the Manager-in-Chief's office, "to be allergic." She leant back in her chair and swung her boots up onto the polished desk. "Imagine sneezing that much!"

"And that's after just *seeing* a rabbit, a whole week ago." Ernest eyed his sister's boot-soles in an unfriendly way. "I dread to think what it'd be like if she actually *bumped into* something furry, up close. People can sneeze themselves to death, you know."

"Did you notice," mused Daisy, twiddling a strand of messy hair, "how she grabbed hold of that suitcase and wouldn't let go of it? That was a bit strange!"

The neatly uniformed boy polished his left cuff link, and sighed.

"For goodness' sake, Daisy," he said. "It's none of our business. Besides, Elsie Tulip is no trouble, if you ask me. I mean, what's a bit of sneezing? If all the Guests we have to look after while Grandmama's away are as easy as this, I think we're going to manage perfectly well, you know."

He headed out of the office, for his usual checks. He had made a habit of taking a short tour of the hotel, at about this time of day, in order to check that all was well. Broken windows had to be pulled shut, cobwebs had to be swept down, and patches of damp had to be observed, in case they were growing any larger. All this took some time, and it was nearly five o'clock when Ernest took the lift to the fourth floor, and listened outside Room 405.

Hardly a sound. Not even a sneeze. Perhaps Elsie Tulip was enjoying a late afternoon nap, Ernest thought, and felt pleased that Oldmoor

Hall had managed to calm her.

Something sharp gripped his shoulder, hard.

"Samson!?"

The parrot. He had landed on his shoulder, dug in his claws, and was giggling in that odd way he had. Perhaps Daisy was right, Ernest thought. Perhaps, despite being Grandmama's dear pet, the bird really was completely crazy.

He continued on his tour, the parrot on his shoulder. The only task that remained was to double-check that the bell on the reception counter was still working, in the unlikely case that another Guest should arrive. Ernest took the lift down to the lobby and stepped out.

Samson saw it first.

But Ernest saw it only a fraction of a second later.

It had just come down the chimney. A cloud

of soot surrounded it, and it was covered in thick black dust.

Tiny eyes blinked. Paws twitched. A fluffy tail stood up, perfectly straight.

A squirrel.

An Unwelcome Visitor

The squirrel was quick. Ernest leapt at the chandelier, threw himself at the mantelpiece but, like a furry bolt of lightning, the little creature flashed away. Ernest tripped over a wastepaper basket, and landed in it, head-first. Furious, he pulled it off and felt the squirrel bounce off his face.

"Come back here!" yelled the Manager-in-Chief.

He lunged again, but the squirrel dodged just as easily, and this time Ernest stumbled into the reception counter and knocked over a bottle of ink, which splattered him with blue spots. The squirrel – and Ernest was sure it was deliberate – bounced off his head again.

"Head Housekeeper!" Ernest dragged himself up, pressed a button on the counter, and spoke into a microphone. "Hurry up with those butterfly nets! Quick!"

She was taking her time, he thought. It had been three-and-a-half minutes at least since he had last spoken to his sister over the hotel announcement system, telling her about the squirrel and ordering her to the Games Room to fetch the nets. What on earth was taking her so long? But even as he thought that, a door burst open on the far side of the lobby and Daisy ran in, out-of-breath and clutching two large nets. Ernest marched across and slammed the door shut behind her.

"For goodness' sake," he snapped. "You can't leave doors open like that. You've got to close them behind you straightaway, or the squirrel'll get out into the hotel, and then we're done for. Understand?"

"If you say so, Ernest!" gasped Daisy. "Now,

where is it?"

Ernest jabbed an arm up at the chandelier. The squirrel had perched there, amongst the glittering glass. Its brown eyes blinked down at the two children.

"Oooh," said Daisy. "It's quite cute, really."

"It is also extremely dangerous for Elsie Tulip!"

Ernest grabbed one of the butterfly nets. "We must get it out of the hotel! 'Look after the Guests', that's what Grandmama said!"

He swiped at the chandelier, but the squirrel jumped away and the net tangled itself up in the dangling glass. Ernest tried to tug it free, furiously.

"Don't just stand there!" he spluttered at Daisy. "You have a go!"

Daisy swiped three times, and accidentally smashed a porcelain ornament, a vase and the clock on the mantelpiece. The squirrel, who had dodged her easily each time, was now perched up on the picture rail, shrieking with triumph. Daisy tossed the net away.

"I don't think butterfly nets work on squirrels," she said.

"Exactly," said Ernest, leaving his net in the chandelier. "Whose stupid idea was it to use them, anyway?"

Daisy was about to point out that it had been *his* idea, that it was his fault not hers, but there was no time. Suddenly, she and her brother were listening to the fireplace.

The sound of scrabbling claws and squeaking voices echoed out of it.

"More of them!"

Ernest grabbed a nearby potted plant and shoved it up the chimney. He used the poker to wedge it into place. The sound of scrabbling and squeaking faded.

"One squirrel is quite enough," he muttered, striding back across the lobby. "If he thinks he's inviting his friends, he can think again."

"It's a bit strange, don't you think?" mused Daisy, staring at the blocked-up fireplace. "I mean, why on earth are there suddenly lots of squirrels? We've never had them before."

"We haven't got time to worry about that," snapped Ernest. "We need another idea, quick." He marched to the counter. "Samson?"

The hotel parrot fluttered down beside him. He had been watching the chase from the top of a bookcase, and had particularly enjoyed it when the children fell over or broke things. He was still cackling with delight.

"Grandmama said we should ask your advice," said Ernest. "So how do we get a squirrel out of the hotel?"

The bird edged along the counter and picked up Ernest's favourite pencil. He began munching it. Perhaps that helped him think, Ernest decided.

"Well?"

The parrot swallowed the rubber on the end

of the pencil with a gulp.

"*Squirrel . . .*"

"Yes?"

"*Worry! Squirrel worry! Worry squirrel!*"

Samson spotted Ernest's second-favourite pencil, and started munching that. Daisy joined her brother, staring at the crazy parrot.

"What on earth does he mean?" puzzled Daisy.

"It's perfectly obvious," said Ernest. He straight-

ened his tie and smoothed his hair. "Leave the squirrel to me. I need you, Head Housekeeper, to go up to our Guest, and tell her not to leave her room. Meet me back here in ten minutes."

"But I still don't understand, Ernest . . ." Daisy was staring at the squirrel, who was trying to dislodge the potted plant from the fireplace with no success. "Why are we being invaded by squirrels in the first place?"

"Will you *stop* distracting me?" Ernest picked up Samson and placed him on his shoulder. "Just warn Elsie Tulip, as I said. Tell her NOT to leave her room. *And, remember, make sure you shut all the doors behind you.*"

He opened a door and slid through it, slamming it quickly behind him so that the squirrel wouldn't get out. Daisy shrugged and, crossing to the other side of the lobby, performed

the same action with a
different door, heading off
into another part of the hotel.

The squirrel gave up on the
poker. It was too firmly jammed
into place. Instead, the furry
creature scampered into the middle of the lobby,
sat up on its haunches, and sniffed the air.

An indignant chatter trilled out of its mouth,
echoing off the marble walls.

Then it carried on scurrying around the room,
seeking for a way, any way at all, to get into the
rest of the hotel.

The Squirrel Worrier

Ernest marched into the library with Samson still on his shoulder. Apart from his office, the library was his favourite room, and it was here that he enjoyed learning the words in the dictionary, as well as reading the many other books in Grandmama's magnificent collection. But there was no time for a quiet read today, he thought, running between the towering bookshelves. Scampering up a ladder, he found the section he wanted: RODENTS.

"Hmm." He flicked through a book. "Any other ideas, Samson? Obviously, the best way to get a squirrel out of the hotel is to *worry* it, to make it *worried* about being there. But how exactly *do* you worry a squirrel, Samson?"

The parrot swooped out of the air, grabbed hold of the page Ernest was reading, tore it out of the book, and flew off, giggling. Ernest swiped at him, and nearly fell off the ladder. That bird really was annoying, he thought, even if he was Grandmama's pet. But then, as he watched the parrot swoop again, he had an idea.

"Hmmm," he said, "interesting."

He slid down the ladder, marched out of the library, and took the lift to the fifth floor. Samson, curious, flapped after him. At the end of a dusty corridor was a door, covered with peeling blue paint. Ernest pushed through it, and breathed in a familiar smell of modelling clay, glue and much-loved toys.

It was the old playroom. He and Daisy had spent almost all their time in it before Grandmama disappeared. The room's musty odour tickled Ernest's nose, nudging distant memories, but he was not here to play now. He went over to the cupboard in the corner and slid open the doors.

Inside were two large model aeroplanes and a remote control unit. Ernest lifted them out and marched back across the room. On his way, he reached into the arts and crafts box and grabbed a handful of elastic bands.

A few seconds later he was in the lift again. Rattling down to the ground floor, he stepped out, clutching everything he had gathered, into the hotel lounge.

On the walls were stuffed heads of various animals, staring down with glass eyes. A wildebeest, a gnu, numerous antelopes and, dangling from the ceiling by a wire . . .

. . . a bald-headed eagle.

"Well done, Manager-in-Chief," Ernest chuckled to himself. "What a clever plan."

Calming Elsie

Daisy tried to tidy her hair, but it was even messier than usual after the squirrel chase. She gave up, and knocked on the door of Room 405.

"Yes?"

The door opened immediately, but only a crack. An eye peered out. It was almost, Daisy thought, as if Elsie had been expecting her.

"I'm afraid there has been a . . . a . . . a . . ."

"Well? Come on! Out with it! Tell me!"

Strange, thought Daisy. She didn't remember Elsie's voice as being quite so shrill. But then she hadn't really heard that much of it, in between the sneezes.

"A furry animal . . . it got in . . . down a

chimney . . ."

"I knew it!" The eye bulged and the voice became a scream. "Didn't I tell you! I'm allergic . . . A-A-A-A-A-CHOOO!"

The sneeze exploded out through the crack in the door, pinning the Head Housekeeper to the opposite side of the corridor. The walls shook. Light bulbs flickered.

"I really am very sorry . . ." Daisy said, edging forward again. "We—"

"Get back! I can smell animal fur on your clothes!" Another sneeze, and Daisy stumbled back again. "You must get rid of it! If it comes near me I'm done for!!"

"We really are doing everything we can, Miss Tulip. Please stay in your room—"

"Of course! I'm not going anywhere! Not with a squirrel on the loose!"

The door slammed. A key turned in the lock. Daisy heard a chair being wedged under the door-handle. Then she made out the sound of sofas, tables and cupboards being dragged across the floor.

"Hmmm," she muttered to herself.

There was something not quite right about this. Slowly, as she stood in the corridor, Daisy worked out what it was.

"How did Elsie Tulip know it was a *squirrel* on the loose?" she muttered. "I didn't say anything about a *squirrel*. I just said it was a *furry animal*."

She continued to hover, and think. Ernest hadn't listened earlier, when she had said how strange it was that squirrels should turn up out of the blue. But it *was* strange. Very strange indeed. A Guest who was incredibly allergic to furry animals had arrived, and *that very same afternoon* a gang of squirrels was trying to break into the hotel.

Most peculiar.

Daisy couldn't help wanting to find out more.

She hurried a little further down the corridor, up to a large potted plant. Pushing her hand into the damp soil, she found a metal lever and pulled it. Next to her, a door clicked open. She stepped into the mouldy darkness and felt her way along the narrow passageway. Her hand made out a button on the wall. She pressed it. Another door slid open.

Daisy was behind a curtain. A curtain with a deliberately placed tattered hole at the same height as her eye. She peered through it . . . into Room 405.

The door was completely barricaded with furniture, and Elsie Tulip was dragging a wardrobe towards the window, to seal that off too. Her plump body strained, her straggly hair flew about, her round face was red with effort.

Then she crouched down by the leather suit-case. The same leather suitcase she had clutched so tightly in the lobby. The suitcase she had refused to let Ernest carry. Her hands crept over it, and she snapped open the fastenings. The lid lifted.

That was all Daisy could see from her hiding place. But she could hear Elsie Tulip's words, drifting across the room.

"Mine . . . Mine . . ."

Daisy edged forward, trying to see more. A floorboard creaked. Elsie looked up.

"Who's there?"

The suitcase slammed shut. Daisy, her heart pounding, slid back into the darkness.

She needed to see Ernest straightaway. Confused thoughts floated in her mind and, although she didn't completely understand what they meant, she wanted to tell her brother about them. Quickly.

She hurried through secret passageways, pushed through spiders' webs and found a spiral staircase. She followed it all the way to the ground floor. It was much quicker to get down to the lobby this way. Her hands closed round another button, and she stepped through another secret door out into the corridor.

WHAM!

She collided straight into the Manager-in-Chief.

Ernest's Clever Plan

"Do be careful, Head Housekeeper!" tutted Ernest, stumbling against the wall. He was carrying a heavy-looking cardboard box with two propellers and a very large beak sticking out of it. "This is valuable equipment, for my extremely clever plan."

"Plan?" Daisy reached into the box and pulled out the stuffed eagle. "What sort of plan uses a stuffed bird and two toy aeroplanes?"

"An extremely clever one, obviously." Ernest snatched the bird back. "Now listen." He placed the box on a table, whipped out a notepad, and began sketching. "Remember Samson's advice?"

"Something about squirrels, and worrying . . ."

"If you want to get rid of a squirrel, you give it something to worry about." Ernest was sketching furiously now. "It'll run off quickly then."

"I see . . ." Daisy scratched her head. "But what *does* a squirrel worry about?"

"Something that might eat it." Ernest drew a picture of the stuffed eagle, and gave it particularly terrifying eyes. "Samson gave me the idea, by swooping at me. A parrot's too small to frighten a squirrel but then I thought, what about

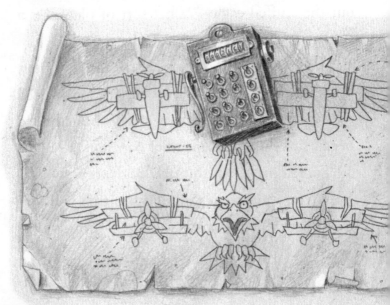

a really big bird? A bird of prey, whose food is little furry creatures. That's when I remembered the bald-headed eagle."

"But this bald-headed eagle," said Daisy, picking it up again and poking her finger into its many moth-holes, "is stuffed. There's nothing very frightening about that."

"It may be stuffed," said Ernest, drawing even faster. "But it's also going to fly." Below the bird,

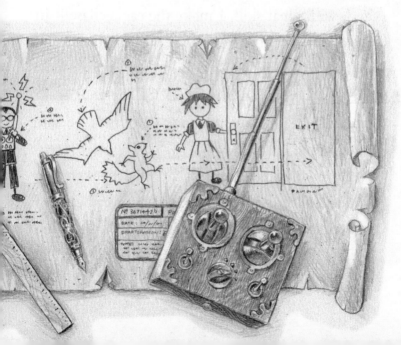

he sketched in the two model aeroplanes, one beneath each wing, and then scribbled in the elastic bands that would hold them in place. "I've checked the power of the engines, weighed the bird, done the calculations: it's all possible. Here's the plan. Using the remote control to guide the planes, I make the bald-headed eagle take off and fly into the lobby. It circles and swoops about. The squirrel sees it, gets scared out of its wits and, with great skill, I make the eagle chase it in the direction of the front door. Which you, Daisy, will OPEN. The squirrel races out and the bird flies out after it. Then you CLOSE the door again and Elsie Tulip, our allergic Guest, will be safe once more!"

Daisy blinked. Ernest had just spoken the oddest collection of words she had ever heard in her life. She had no idea what to say. At the same time, she remembered why she had run back down to find him.

"There's something I need to tell you, Ernest. About Elsie."

"Not now, Head Housekeeper." Ernest picked up the cardboard box and headed down the corridor towards the lobby. "I need to check how high the lobby roof is, in order to plan the eagle's flight."

"But Ernest—"

Ernest walked faster. How annoying his sister could be. He had just explained an extremely clever plan to her, and all she wanted to do was talk about something else. It was typical.

He threw open the door to the lobby, and marched in . . .

With disastrous results.

Oops!

Ernest remembered the instructions he had given the Head Housekeeper, about using the doors into the lobby. Close the door as soon as you are through, he had said, or the squirrel will get into the main part of the hotel. Such *clear* instructions. He remembered them perfectly.

Unfortunately, he also remembered them a little too late.

He left the door of the lobby open. He felt a fluffy tail tickle past his ear. The squirrel had raced out of the foyer, up into the hotel.

Ernest froze. What could he do to rescue this dreadful situation? But then, things got even worse because Daisy, still talking about Elsie, walked straight into her

brother's back . . . and sent the box he
was holding flying out of his arms.

Ernest's mouth dropped open. Daisy's eyes
bulged.

The box flew through the air, then hit the
floor and skidded across the marble. It collided
into the fireplace and knocked away the poker.
The plant pot collapsed out of the chimney and
rolled away.

Little paws scuttled. Soot trickled out of the
fireplace and spilled onto the floor.

Out they came, a blizzard of squirrels. There
must have been twenty of them, maybe thirty.
Ernest and Daisy lost count. The squirrels raced
between the children's legs and around their feet,
chattering with excitement.

Then they disappeared through the still-open
door, out into the hotel.

An Argument

"That was your fault!" said Ernest furiously, straightening his tie before grabbing the box from the fireplace. "You walked into me!"

"You shouldn't carry around boxes of junk!" Daisy pointed indignantly at the box. "Accidents are bound to happen!"

"It is *not* a box of junk." Ernest gritted his teeth. "It is a box full of clever equipment, for a clever plan, as I have already explained."

There was more scrabbling from the chimney. Ernest grabbed the potted plant again and shoved it back up, this time securing it with two pokers. Hearing the sound of tiny paws scuttling back up the chimney, he crossed to the front door, flipped open the spyhole, and peered out.

"Crumbs," he muttered. "We're surrounded."

Another gang of squirrels, forty or fifty of them, were scuttling around in the swirling fog. Ernest stared at them before being rudely elbowed out of the way by Daisy, who wanted to look for herself.

"There's definitely something VERY odd about this," she muttered.

She told Ernest everything she had been thinking – about the strangeness of so many squirrels arriving at almost the exact same time as an allergic Guest. She also mentioned that she'd been spying on Elsie, in her room.

"You spied on a Guest?" gasped Ernest, shocked.

"Of course," shrugged Daisy. "That's when I saw her opening the suitcase. You know, I'm sure that's got something to do with it as well, Ernest.

I mean, why didn't she let you carry it? It's a bit strange, don't you think?"

"No," said Ernest, marching across the lobby, clutching his equipment. "Head Housekeeper, all I am thinking about is how to look after our Guest. That's what Grandmama told us to do, isn't it?" He turned and saluted the picture of the old woman on the wall. "That's why I'm going to carry out my brilliant plan."

"But your plan's no good now, is it?" Daisy ran after her brother. "I suppose it *might* have worked, when it was just one squirrel trapped here in the lobby with nowhere else to go. But now there are loads of squirrels, and they'll be all over the hotel by now!"

"My plan *will* work," said Ernest, marching down the corridor. "It will work *perfectly* well."

He reached the main stairwell and stared up.

Above him was a blur of squirrels, bushy tails curling, furry bodies leaping, as the little creatures hurtled around the spiralling banisters, dashing this way and that along the corridors. But this only made Ernest more determined that his plan would succeed.

"You'll see, Head Housekeeper," he said. "Before long, this hotel will be squirrel-free. Our Guest will be safe. All you need to do is go back to the lobby, stand by the front door, wait for every single squirrel to come racing towards you, chased by a bald-headed eagle. Open the door, then close it when they've left. Understand? Good."

He marched off down the corridor and stomped into the lift, leaving Daisy to stare up at the acrobatic squirrels.

What are they doing here? she thought. It couldn't be just bad luck that they had turned up at the same time as Elsie. *Could it?* Something was going on, she was sure of it. *But what?*

Slowly, she made her way back to the lobby, and took up her position by the front door. Her brother's plan was a peculiar one, but at least he *had* a plan. She just had a hunch, a strange feeling that something wasn't quite right. She should probably just forget all about it, she told herself.

But that was impossible. She had never been so curious about anything in her life. Her brain felt as if a bottle of fizzy drink had been poured into it, leaving it trembling and popping with strange possibilities.

She stood by the front door, ready to open it when the time came . . .

. . . and continued to think.

The Flight of the Bald-headed Eagle

Ernest was in his office. He reached into a drawer of his desk and took out a screwdriver. Nimbly, he tightened a few screws on the two aeroplanes and then, with an expert flick of elastic bands, he attached each plane to one of the stuffed eagle's wings. He reached for the screwdriver again, only to discover that Samson had stolen it, and he spent the next two minutes chasing after the giggling parrot to get it back. A few more adjustments, then he picked up the remote control. With a final flourish, he pulled out an old pair of leather flying goggles, and snapped them onto his face. He was ready.

Striding out of his office, he spotted a squirrel

at the end of the corridor. He pressed himself into the doorway, out of its sight. Holding up the stuffed eagle, he jiggled the joystick on the remote control.

The propellers whirred. The bird wobbled out into the corridor.

Almost immediately, Ernest heard a chatter of fright and, peering out, he saw that the little rodent had taken off, terrified by what it had seen. His plan had begun. He followed the stuffed eagle as it flew along the corridor. "Squirrels are very intelligent animals", the book in the library had said. If one of them saw a bird of prey flying around the hotel, it would tell the others. Word would spread. Ernest hurried after the bird, guiding it with the remote control, and saw another squirrel dash off in fright, then another. Finally, he turned a corner and emerged at the top of the main stairwell.

How proud Grandmama would be.

Word *had* spread. The squirrels were streaming out of every corridor of the hotel, emptying into the stairwell, chattering frantically about what they had seen. But their worries were only just beginning, Ernest thought to himself. And he just couldn't help giving a little chuckle, as he flicked a switch and sent the eagle hovering out into the stairwell.

The squirrels looked up, and saw it.

Ernest had never seen such speed. The squirrels flashed off down the stairway,

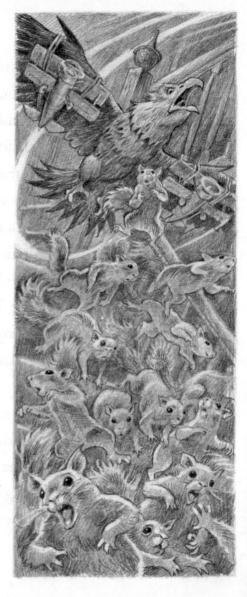

squeaking with terror. The neatly uniformed boy was chuckling quite loudly now, as he hopped up onto the polished banister and slid down it, the remote control still in his hands. He slid all the way down to the bottom, leaping off and landing on his feet just as the squirrels – a panicking crowd of fluffy tails and jabbering teeth – hurtled off the stairs and raced towards the lobby.

The Manager-in-Chief giggled with delight. Now was the moment. His thumbs twiddled the levers and the mighty eagle flew. With the help of this *magnificent* bird, he would chase the troublesome rodents into the lobby and right out of the front door.

The front door that Daisy would be standing by.

Wouldn't she?

Ernest stepped into the lobby. His mouth dropped open, with sheer astonishment.

The front door was closed. Daisy was nowhere to be seen.

The awful thing, he thought, was that the plan was going so well. The eagle was chasing the squirrels towards the front door, and the squirrels were desperately trying to get through it, scrabbling at the hinges or trying to squeeze through the letterbox. They were terrified of the cruel bird of prey that was swooping towards them. But they wouldn't be for long.

BANG! The bald-headed eagle slammed into the back of the door. It exploded into a mass of feathers, propellers and stuffing. The eagle's beak lodged itself in a lampshade. Everything else dropped down onto the doormat. One of the bird's glass eyes rolled across the floor, right up to one of the squirrels, who picked it up and examined it. Then he showed it to his friends, who all began to chatter with puzzlement.

Ernest collapsed. Every gram of strength had suddenly left him at the failure, the utter failure, of his brilliant plan. Staring up at the lobby walls, he caught sight of Grandmama's portrait, but looked away, ashamed. He couldn't bear to see that kind face, whom he had failed so terribly.

He closed his eyes and sighed.

Curiouser and Curiouser

Ernest was going to be cross, Daisy thought, as she raced along the secret passage. In fact, he was going to go completely crazy.

But she hadn't been able to stop herself. That fizzing in her brain had got fizzier and fizzier until she just *had* to find out what was going on. Anyway, there was always a slight chance that she might carry out *her* plan and get back in time to help with the front door. But she had to be quick.

She had raced out of the lobby, opened the secret door nearby, and had been in such a rush that she hadn't even bothered to close it behind her. Now she was hurtling along the dark passageway, corkscrewing up the spiral staircase, until she reached Room 405.

The secret door was still open, and the tapestry with the hole in it fluttered. But there was no time for spying now. The Head Housekeeper flung the tapestry to one side and stomped into Elsie's room.

"Miss Tulip?"

Elsie was still hunched over the leather suitcase. But as soon as she saw Daisy, she slammed the case shut and leapt up.

"What are you doing here? Get back down there and stop those squirrels! Have you forgotten that I'm highly allergic to them? The slightest whiff of squirrel fur . . ."

But Daisy didn't move. She folded her arms and planted her feet firmly on the carpet.

"It's a bit odd, don't you think, Miss Tulip, that all these squirrels have turned up here? *On the very same day* you happened to arrive with your strange allergy?"

The question had an extraordinary effect. Elsie Tulip stumbled backwards, clutching the suitcase, and knocked a lamp off the table, smashing it. Daisy's remark seemed to have completely thrown her. She stumbled around a bit more, smashing a few things, before finally being able to reply.

"Odd? I don't think so! It's just bad luck,

that's all . . ."

The suitcase, Daisy thought. That was at the bottom of it all. She had never seen anyone clutch an item of luggage so tightly. With every second that went by, Elsie seemed to be clutching it even harder, her arms quivering, her knuckles white.

"I don't suppose," Daisy said, twiddling a strand of her tangled hair, "that you might have something *in* that suitcase? Something that might explain it all?"

This question had an even more extraordinary effect. Elsie Tulip froze, her face turning bright red, dribbles of perspiration sliding down her forehead. Suddenly, she looked as guilty as a cat who had been discovered half-way through swallowing a budgerigar. She gripped the suitcase harder than ever.

"Please don't make me give them back! Please!

I beg you!"

"Give *them* back? Give what back?" Daisy thought frantically about why Elsie would say such a thing, and then gasped with astonishment. "You haven't . . . *stolen* something, have you?"

Elsie was in a panic now. She hurled herself towards the door and tried to get out, but realised it would take too long to pull away all the furniture she had piled against it. Desperately, she looked for another way out of the room.

It was too late. Daisy had grabbed hold of the suitcase. Elsie yelped, and the two of them stood struggling, the suitcase lurching between them.

"You've stolen something that belongs to those squirrels, haven't you!" Daisy squealed. "That's why they've come here! To get back whatever's in this suitcase!"

"YES!" wailed Elsie Tulip. "I mean, NO!"

Follow Those Squirrels

Ernest opened his eyes. He had heard something. The squirrels seemed to have heard something too.

Their ears were pricked up. From far away, voices floated into the lobby. They seemed to be arguing about something. Ernest recognised Daisy's squeaky tones, and the squirrels, it seemed, recognised the other voice.

Elsie Tulip.

The squirrels shot off. They flew across the lobby floor, their claws skittering over the marble. Ernest scrambled up.

"Come back!"

His plan had failed. But the least he could do was to stop those dreadful creatures reaching the poor allergic Guest. He stumbled into the corridor, and saw just one last tail disappearing through the secret door that Daisy had left open. He ran through the door and stared into the gloom.

No time to be afraid, he told himself. Despite what he'd told Daisy, he was indeed very scared of the dark. That was why he had never wanted to explore the hotel's secret passages with her, if he could possibly help it.

But this was a desperate situation. Bravely, he plunged in. He could hear the squirrels, chattering ahead of him, as he lurched after them. Spiders' webs covered his face, and he was sure he felt a spider scurry up his nose, but he sneezed it out. He tripped several times, walked into a wall once, then stumbled back and fell through more cobwebs. He clambered up a spiral staircase. However scared he was, he told himself, he must keep going.

"BOO!"

It was Samson, flapping in his face, giggling as usual. He really was very irritating, Ernest thought, and pushed past him. Ahead was a rectangle of light, and he saw another fluffy tail disappearing through it. He ran the last few metres and was greeted by the worst sight that he, the Manager-in-Chief of Oldmoor Hall, had ever seen.

He was in Room 405. He recognised the carpet, the furniture, the window, everything. In the middle of that room stood Elsie, whom he knew, whom he knew for a *fact*, was allergic to anything furry.

She was covered in SQUIRRELS.

The Suitcase

The squirrels swarmed over Elsie. A fluffy tail quivered under her nose like a large moustache. Ernest closed his eyes.

"Forgive me, Grandmama," he muttered.

"Help me, Ernest! Don't just stand there!"

Ernest flicked his eyes back open and saw Daisy. For some reason, she was grappling with Elsie's suitcase, trying to wrestle it away from the squirrel-covered Guest.

"What on earth are you doing, Head Housekeeper? Put that suitcase down! A Guest's luggage is private!"

"You don't understand, Ernest!" Daisy tugged harder. "I've worked out what's going on!"

"It's perfectly obvious what's going on!"

spluttered Ernest. "We have failed to look after our Guest! She is allergic to furry animals, and now she is covered with squirrels! She'll probably sneeze herself to death!"

"But that's another thing!" Daisy continued to tug. "Haven't you noticed?" She took a huge breath. "Elsie isn't sneezing!"

Daisy had been doing a lot of suitcase-tugging since she had burst into Elsie's room. But she had also been doing a lot of looking around and thinking. She'd noticed that Elsie was, indeed, *not sneezing*. Instead, she seemed to be putting all her effort into getting her suitcase back, while the squirrels shrieked around her.

"I don't understand," protested Ernest. "She's allergic to furry things!"

"That's what she told us, Ernest!" Daisy lurched into a table and smashed a vase. "But what if . . .

82

she *isn't* allergic?"

"*Isn't* allergic? But she sneezed all over me!"

"Ah, but what if she was just *pretending* to be allergic?" Daisy tripped over a potted plant and kept tugging. "What if she just wanted us to *think* she was allergic? So that we would do everything we could to stop the squirrels getting to her?"

"But . . ." Ernest saw his face in one of the room's mirrors and thought it had never looked so bewildered. "Why?"

"*Because she's stolen something that belongs to those squirrels!*" Daisy's face was bright red, partly because of the tugging, but mostly because of the strain of working things out. "*Something that's inside this suitcase!*"

"Stolen something from squirrels?" gasped Ernest. "But what could that possibly be?"

Just then, a terrible groan crawled out of Elsie's throat. The squirrels were nibbling at the hand that gripped the suitcase, and she flailed at them with the other, but her strength had gone. The suitcase flew through the air, slammed into the wall, sprang open and . . .

Out rattled hundreds of round, brown nuts.

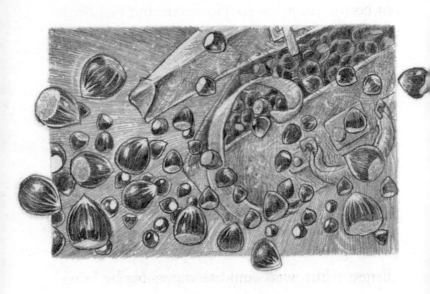

What Elsie Did

The nuts bounced off the walls, the ceiling and the floor. They were as hard as bullets. The squirrels were like bullets too, flashing around the room at impossible speeds, snatching up their precious objects. In just a few seconds, every nut had been grabbed from wherever it had landed. Some had even been caught in mid-air. Then the squirrels had swept off through the secret passage, disappearing into the darkness.

For a while, everyone was too surprised, shocked and exhausted to say anything. But finally, Daisy broke the silence.

"You stole the squirrels' nuts!" she gasped, pointing at Elsie. "AND you pretended to be allergic, so that we would stop the squirrels getting to you!"

"It's true!" Elsie sobbed, collapsing onto the floor, still clutching the open suitcase. "I'm sorry I fibbed! But I had to! You would never have helped me if you knew the truth!"

"We certainly wouldn't have!" Daisy was pacing across the room. "You're a thief! Those poor squirrels!" She marched over to Ernest. "It all makes sense! Even Samson's crazy advice makes sense. *Worry . . . Squirrels . . .* Well, the squirrels *were* worried! They were worried about their nuts!"

"*Correct!*" cawed Samson. He had been perched on the wardrobe, enjoying the suitcase fight, but now he cackled with laughter and fell upside-down into the wastepaper bin. "*Squirrel worry!*"

"I don't believe it!" Ernest glared at Elsie. "You sneezed all over me when you arrived! I thought

you couldn't help yourself, but in fact you were just pretending!"

"I had to!" wailed Elsie. "I had to make you think I was *really* allergic! So you'd work as hard as you could to protect me from those squirrels!" She took out her pink-spotted handkerchief into which she had pretended to sneeze so many times, and buried her sobbing face in it. "But the squirrels got their nuts in the end!"

"I don't understand." Ernest started to pace like his sister. "Why steal nuts? You can buy nuts anywhere!"

"Ah, but only the best nuts will do for me!" sobbed Elsie. "I happen to be a world-famous nut collector, you see! For many years now, I have been collecting the world's most delicious nuts! I'll stop at nothing to get my hands on them!" Another sob. "That's why I started getting involved with squirrels. Because every nut collector knows that the best nuts are always the ones the squirrels get!"

"Really?" Ernest was genuinely interested in this fact. "I never knew that!"

"It's obvious!" From a pocket inside the suitcase, Elsie pulled out a tattered old book. *Nuts of the World* it said on the cover, and she flicked

through it. "No matter how quick we humans are, the squirrels will always get to a nut tree first. They pick the most delicious nuts and hoard them away. Every nut collector dreams of stealing squirrels' nuts. I've been trying for years. But it's incredibly difficult. Squirrels guard their nuts carefully, you see."

"How did you manage it?" Ernest enquired.

"With a fake nut and a vacuum cleaner," replied Elsie, snapping the book shut. "I followed those squirrels back to the oak tree where they kept their nuts in a hollow. Then, I glued an extremely large and delicious-looking fake nut to another tree, on the other side of the forest. A few squirrels went off, to try to get this fake nut, but I'd used very strong glue, so the rest of the squirrels had to go and help so they could all pull together to get the nut. Which meant there were no squirrels left

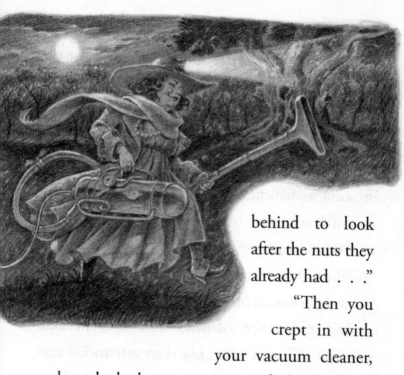

behind to look after the nuts they already had . . ."

"Then you crept in with your vacuum cleaner, and sucked those nuts out of the hollow." Daisy's voice was stern and accusing. "Those poor squirrels."

"Any nut collector would have done the same!" Elsie's plump body crumpled. "And what do you mean, poor squirrels? Poor me! Ever since, those ruthless little rodents have been chasing me! I've been on the run! I thought that maybe, here in this hotel, I might have escaped them . . . but it was not to be!"

"Why on earth didn't you gobble the nuts up, as soon as you stole them?" said Ernest. "That way, it'd be too late for the squirrels to chase you!"

"*Gobble them up?*" Elsie looked utterly outraged. "Are you crazy? I've waited all my life to get my hands on a bunch of nuts like these! I'm not going to just gulp them down!" Her eyes became suddenly dreamy. "No, my plan was to eat just one nut a year, on my birthday. I would have served it on a silver plate, with a glass of the very finest chilled white wine to go with it . . ." Another sob exploded out of her. "But that's not going to happen now, is it? Those squirrels have hunted me down! They've got their nuts back! And left me with nothing! Nothing!"

Just then, there was a tap at the window.

A squirrel was sitting on the sill outside. A single paw tapped at the glass.

"What's it doing?" spluttered Elsie. "It's got what it wanted! Can't it leave me in peace?"

But Daisy noticed something. She stepped across to the window and rattled it up. The squirrel hopped inside.

From inside its cheeks, out popped a single, perfectly round nut.

The squirrel placed it on the carpet, in front of Daisy's boots.

It squeaked in a friendly way.

Then it hopped back out through the window, into the misty morning.

An Act of Kindness

"I can't believe it!" Elsie's tear-stained eyes bulged. "A squirrel giving up one of its nuts? Unheard of!" She lunged across the carpet, her plump fingers reaching. "Give it to me!"

"I *don't* think so." Daisy snatched up the nut. "The squirrel gave it to me, not you!"

"But why?" wailed Elsie. "I don't understand!"

"Hang on a minute." Ernest had been standing perfectly still since the extraordinary moment with the squirrel. He was deep in thought. "What if the squirrels are saying *thank you* to the Head Housekeeper?" He started pacing again. "If it hadn't been for her, they might never have got their nuts back. But they did. Perhaps, in return for her act of kindness, they're giving her a present?"

"That's the most ridiculous thing I've ever heard!" Elsie spluttered. "They're just dumb animals, you know."

"In fact, squirrels are quite intelligent," said Ernest, remembering the book he'd read in the library. "After all, dogs love their owners and do tricks for them. Cats like their owners too, and bring little dead mice to them as gifts. Why shouldn't squirrels do something a bit like it?"

Elsie blinked. She thought about what Ernest had said.

"An act of kindness . . ." she mused. "Do you seriously think that if you do something kind to them, the squirrels will give you a nut, as some sort of . . . present?"

"That's *exactly* what he's saying!" Daisy tossed her nut triumphantly in the air. "It's a lot easier than trying to steal them with a fake nut and a vacuum cleaner!"

"What we need to work out," said Ernest, pacing so fast he became a blur. "Is how you, Elsie Tulip, can do an act of kindness for these squirrels. Maybe if you did, just maybe . . ." He turned, shrugged. "They'd give you a nut too?"

"A nut?" Elsie's eyes shone with hope. "But how? I haven't got the faintest idea how to be kind to squirrels! All I know is how to steal from them!"

"We need to find something the squirrels need," muttered Daisy. "If you could help them, then that'd be an act of kindness, wouldn't it?"

"But what *do* squirrels need?" Elsie looked utterly bewildered. "What? I don't understand . . ."

But even as she tried to stutter out a few

more baffled words, her speech was silenced by a loud rattling noise, like hailstones falling from the sky.

Rat-A-Tat-Tat

Ernest and Daisy stuck their heads out of the window and found themselves staring through the fog into a downpour of nuts. Ernest peered up and saw a row of squirrels on the roof, hurling their precious nuts down to the ground.

"What's going on?" he said.

"They're trying to crack them!" Elsie thrust her head out of the window. "Now they've got them back, they want to crack them and eat them!"

She was right, although the squirrels didn't seem to be having much luck. Some were throwing the nuts down at the hotel's concrete front steps, a long way below, but the nuts were bouncing off, unbroken. Other squirrels were

retrieving them, carrying them back up the drainpipes and along the guttering, to be thrown from the roof again.

"Looks like a lot of work," Ernest mused.

"It is!" cried Elsie. "It can sometimes take squirrels a whole day of chiselling, gnawing or throwing nuts from high places before they manage to crack any! But they have to do it! What's inside is so delicious, you see!"

Ernest stared back up at the roof and the furry creatures lined up along it. How determined they looked, he thought. But also, perhaps, a little exhausted.

"It's not much of a life, is it?" he mused. "Collecting nuts. Guarding them. Then having to work non-stop trying to crack them. Rather tiring, if you ask me."

"I suppose so," muttered Elsie. "I'd never really

thought about it."

Something occurred to the Manager-in-Chief as he pulled himself back in through the window.

"How were *you* going to crack the nuts, Miss Tulip?" he asked. "Every year, on your birthday?"

"With this!" Elsie reached a hand into her coat, and pulled out something heavy and mechanical. "A steel nutcracker! It splinters the shells in seconds! With just a squeeze!"

She dropped it into Ernest's hands. Daisy sidled up next to him, and together the two children stared at the gleaming metal device.

"What?" cried Elsie, unnerved by the way they had both gone silent. "WHAT?"

Ernest looked at Daisy. Daisy looked at Ernest.

"I think," said Ernest. "We have an idea."

Elsie Cracks Up

"It's perfectly simple," said Ernest, smoothing his hair. "You, Elsie Tulip, are going to do something kind for the squirrels. They are going to give you nuts in return."

"But what is this kind thing?" wailed Elsie. "I don't understand . . ."

"Crack the squirrels' nuts for them!" said Daisy, tossing her the nutcracker. "They'll be ever so grateful."

She leant out of the window and whistled. Immediately, a curious squirrel appeared on the sill. Daisy held up the nut she had been given, making sure the squirrel had seen it. Then she tossed it over to Elsie.

Elsie, still looking puzzled, did as she was told.

She slipped the nut into the cracker and, with a quick squeeze, cracked it.

The squirrel blinked. It had clearly never seen a nut cracked so quickly. But it had an even bigger surprise coming.

"Go on, Miss Tulip," Ernest said. "Give it the cracked nut. An act of kindness, remember?"

For a few seconds, Elsie hesitated. She held up the inside bit of the nut, round and sweet, and sniffed it, drool glistening at the corner of her

mouth. But then she did as she was told. She tossed the precious item straight into the squirrel's paws.

It gobbled it up. And shot out the window.

"So much for that then," sniffed Elsie. "It just snaffled it and ran off."

"Wait," said Ernest, polishing his cuff links. "Squirrels are highly intelligent, remember. Word will spread, of your act of kindness. Word will spread."

"Look!" squealed Daisy, pointing at the window.

The squirrel had returned. With it were three of its friends, each of whom, Ernest observed,

was clutching a nut.

"They've understood!" he exclaimed.

"May I?" said Daisy to the squirrels, holding out a hand. The three rodents hesitated, and then dropped their nuts into her palm. She, in turn, tossed them over to Elsie who, still a little uncertain, cracked them. A few seconds later, the squirrels were gobbling up their nuts.

"Do you think I've been kind enough yet?" muttered Elsie. "My wrist's getting tired, with all this cracking."

But Elsie's work had only just begun. The window was crowded with squirrels now. Ernest watched them hand their nuts to Daisy, who threw them over to Elsie, who cracked them and tossed them back to the squirrels. Nearly half an hour later, the pile of broken shells reached up to Elsie's knees.

"I must have cracked every single nut there is!" she wailed, rubbing her aching wrist as the last squirrel disappeared off the window sill. "And for what?"

Then, something extraordinary happened.

A squirrel hopped in through the window and landed on the carpet by Elsie's feet. In its paws, it clutched a final nut. It jumped over and dropped it into Elsie's lap.

"Oh, I suppose I could manage one more," sighed Elsie. She cracked the nut, and held out the sweet round inside bit.

But the squirrel was gone.

"It's for you, Elsie," whispered Daisy. "It's a present, to thank you for your act of kindness."

"Are you sure?" Elsie's lips quivered with emotion. "It's really for me?"

"Eat it," said Ernest. "I know it's not your birthday, but if you ask me, there's plenty to celebrate."

Elsie did as she was told. She popped it into her mouth. Her teeth crunched the nut slowly.

Tears of delight sprinkled from her eyes.

As he watched those tears slide down Elsie's cheeks, Ernest found himself sliding too. He was sliding down into a nearby chair. Suddenly, he was feeling unbelievably tired. It was as if all the frantic activities of the day – nets, nuts, aeroplanes, squirrels and a bald-headed eagle – were catching up with him. That was no excuse, of course. The Guest was still in the hotel, and so it was his duty to look after her.

That was what Grandmama had asked.

But still, just a quick snooze, he thought. If anything else needed to be done, the Head

Housekeeper could probably manage it on her own.

He closed his eyes.

A Satisfied Guest

The breakfast tray rattled down on Ernest's bed. His eyes flickered open, and he saw his sister pouring him a cup of tea with one hand. On the nearby wall, a telephone was ringing.

"Wakey, wakey," Daisy said. "I think you'd better answer that."

Ernest stumbled out of bed. He looked down and saw that he was still in his uniform, which was looking rather crumpled.

"How long have I been asleep, Head Housekeeper?"

"Fourteen hours." Daisy shrugged. "I tucked you in after you fainted. That was yesterday evening and it's morning now." The telephone jangled.

"Anyway, are you going to take that call or not?"

Ernest picked up the receiver. Still waking up, he pressed it to his ear.

"Hello?"

"*I followed them!*" Elsie's voice crackled and popped, with sheer delight. "*I followed them all night!*"

"I beg your pardon?" mumbled Ernest.

"It's true," butted in Daisy, who could hear Elsie's voice loud and clear. "After you collapsed, the squirrels left the hotel. She raced off with them!"

"*And now I'm here!*" The voice continued to crackle, and Ernest made out the noise of shrieking squirrels in the background. "*In this simply wonderful forest!*"

"Forest?"

"*The squirrels led me to it!*" Elsie giggled. "*To a tree right in the middle of it! And another collection of nuts! I'm cracking them for my little furry friends right now!*"

"And saving a few for yourself, of course," Daisy added, leaning into the receiver.

"*Of course!*" squealed the voice. "*That's all part of the agreement! And another thing . . .*"

"Yes?" murmured Ernest, still a little sleepy, and trying to keep up.

"*We're only just beginning!*" crackled the voice. "*The squirrels and I, we have decided to travel the world! In search of other far-off forests, full of nuts! The squirrels will gather them! I will crack! Together, we will be the happiest nut collectors there have ever been!*"

Ernest felt something twitch against his left hand. Looking down, he saw it was Daisy. She was reaching for his hand.

"Well done, Ernest," she whispered.

"Well done, Daisy," he whispered back.

Because it didn't really matter, he told himself, about everything else. Who had understood what, done what, messed up what – that was all in the past now. Their Guest was happy. Not only that, but the squirrels were as well.

"Well, it does sound as though things have worked out very nicely, Ms Tulip," said Ernest, into the phone. "For both you, and the squirrels."

"*It's all down to you!*" squealed the happy voice. "*And to Oldmoor Hall! What a marvellous hotel! Thank you!*" The squirrels squealed in the background, saying something that would probably, Ernest thought, be Squirrel-eze for thank you. "*Goodbye!*"

The phone went dead. Ernest dropped the receiver onto its cradle. He was properly awake now.

"A satisfied Guest," he murmured. "Who would have thought it?"

Goodbye, Elsie

The two children stepped out onto the rickety balcony. Daisy peered through the telescope, out into the fog. In particular, she studied the lonely road leading away from Oldmoor Hall.

"Any sign of the next one?" asked Ernest.

"Nope," said Daisy. She lowered the telescope. "You know, we really didn't do too badly. Elsie Tulip was our very first guest, after all. And a rather strange one."

"Indeed," said Ernest.

He was deep in thought. Plumes of fog coiled around him, and up in the sky the sun struggled to shine through the gloom. Ernest mused. And mused again.

What if all the Guests were as strange as Elsie? What if some of them were even stranger? How would he and the Head Housekeeper deal with them? It really would have been helpful if Grandmama had told them a little bit more about this hotel, and the Guests who came to stay in it. Even the tiniest scrap of information would have been useful . . .

Enough, he told himself. What Grandmama *hadn't* said wasn't important. It was what she *had* said. That was what mattered.

"Take charge of the hotel. Look after the Guests." From his jacket pocket, Ernest took half of the postcard on which Grandmama's message had been written. He noticed that Daisy had taken out her half too, and they held the two pieces together, making it whole.

"Do you think . . ." Ernest whispered, "that

Grandmama will come back soon?"

"I don't know, Ernest," said Daisy. "It's a mystery."

The fog swirled. The rickety hotel creaked. The children shivered.

"But I'll tell you one thing," Daisy continued. "I bet, when she does eventually get back, she'll be really pleased with how we've managed. Oh yes, and one more thing."

"What?" Ernest turned to face his sister. For some reason, she was grinning. "What's so funny?"

"You've got a parrot on your head."

The Manager-in-Chief's eyes swivelled up and he saw Samson, hovering over him. The bird was giggling. He'd clearly been making funny faces at the Head Housekeeper throughout the serious conversation that had just taken place.

"Drat that bird," giggled Daisy.

"For once, Head Housekeeper," said Ernest, as he brushed the parrot away, sending him flying into the mist. "I agree with you entirely."

The two children turned and stepped off the balcony, back into Oldmoor Hall.

And began to get ready . . .

. . . for the next Guest.

OLDMOOR HALL

Thank you for visiting.
We hope to see you again soon!